Flash

Science
Fiction
For Kids

An Anthology

Compiled
by
Ken Stiles, Ed.

"Nothing has to be true, but everything has to sound true."

- Isaac Asimov, *Second Foundation*

The 100-word very short stories (called drabbles) are written by Justin Lowmaster

All stories are copyrighted by their respective authors. Used by permission.

Introduction

What is flash fiction? Flash fiction is a term coined recently and basically means a very short story. Though the number of words tends to differ with every author, the word count is typically between 100 – 1500 words. Though traditional stories were longer, the Internet has revolutionized reading and now is all about blurbs. So, what is flash fiction exactly?

Like every other story, flash fiction should have a beginning, story line and ending. But with flash fiction, there's no time to build-up the story line, or the characters. Usually, the whole story revolves around one powerful event. A beautiful sunset, or a chaotic earthquake street, a war zone, or whatever!

Flash fiction, then, is a short form of storytelling. The stories use powerful images and quick action to make the stories enjoyable and memorable.

Enjoy this collection of flash fiction science fiction stories and fill those brief moments of time with good old-fashioned fun.

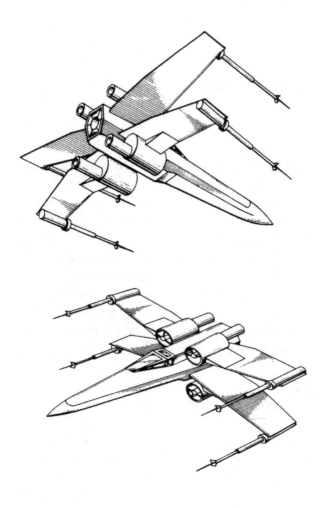

Table of Contents

Fancy Dinner

Emmaline sat at the giant octagonal table. She felt like a princess. Her father had said she wasn't a princess because he wasn't a king, but things were going to get a lot fancier now that he was an ambassador to the Galactic Council. She stared at the utensils surrounding her plate at odd angles. That one might be a fork. Do aliens pick silverware from the outside in? Wary of starting an interstellar war, she carefully touched the outermost fork like object. A tall, purple-furred waiter leaned over.

"Dear child, those are for decoration only. Use your fingers, please."

Dishwashing Is Fun

Mother ate the last of her mashed potatoes.

"OK, whose turn is it to clean the dishes?"

Jeremy and Sarah jumped up. "It's my turn!" they shouted.

Father grinned. "Wasn't like this when I was a kid."

Sarah shoved Jeremy. "You did them last time."

"No I didn't!"

Mother stood. "Both of you stop, or I'm going to clean them."

Both children protested. Father stood. "OK, Jeremy, you do the cooking dishes, Sarah, the ones from the table."

"I'm first!" Jeremy shouted and ran. Sonic blaster in hand, he giggled as bits of food wiggled and fell from the dishes.

The Football Gizmo

by C. William Russette 2011

Alec opened the garage door and to no surprise it was as black as the rest of the house. Only his flashlight, smart phone and watch provided illumination. He removed his headphones and threw them over one shoulder.

"Dad! Where's the power?" Alec said.

It was strange how quiet the garage was. There was always the sound of something his father was working on. Some machine that could control all the windows and doors in the house or a more efficient blender for Mom or the microwave dryer. If something wasn't rattling around the garage, then Alec would hear Dad's ancient music that he called rock and roll.

So old school, Alec thought. He swept the flashlight over the interior of the garage. Where was Dad? He wouldn't have blown the power to the house and then bailed. He never had, anyway. Mom would have roasted him. She's at work though and Alec saw his Dad's car in the driveway on his way back here.

"Dad? Where are you?"

No answer.

Alec walked down the carpeted stairs to the garage floor. The circuit breaker was on the far side of the 'lab' as his father called it. It wasn't a garage anymore. There was no room for a car with all the engines, generators, capacitors and whatever else his Dad made.

It was obvious which breaker was tripped even if Alec hadn't already handled such an emergency a hundred times. Most twelve year olds couldn't even find the circuit box never mind reset the switch.

Alec did so. The lab thrummed back to life. For a second he was worried he might find his Dad's body, the result of some grizzly accident. No mess, nothing burnt, and no Dad either. There was something though.

On the main work bench sat a contraption that Alec had never seen before. It was roughly in the shape of a football. Had there been any kind of covering on it that is. This thing was all wires, tubing, circuits and other things Alec had never seen before.

"What is this?"

There were only a few wires leading away from it. One was for power, one led to a computer tower and another to a keyboard. The monitor came on and began running through a sequence of routines and sub-routines that made no sense. When it stopped, the bottom of the screen read:

SYSTEM READY
TEST RUN 1 SUCCESSFUL
TEST RUN 2 CONDITIONS OPTIMAL
PRESS ENTER WHEN READY

Alec looked around the garage. Still no Dad. What was Dad working on that made him run off so suddenly? He looked around for something that seemed like a gun or a laser barrel. Alec felt dumb when he did it but he couldn't stop himself. Dad didn't work with lasers so there is no way that he could have disintegrated himself.

There would have been some kind of smell and the lab smelled normal.

So where was Dad?

Alec picked up the football-gadget. It was pretty light.

His eyes roamed the space before him.

"Dad? Mind if I try your new thingy here? It says it's ready."

Nothing.

"Say something if you don't want me to mess with it!"

Still nothing.

"Well, he never said I couldn't," Alec said and pressed enter.

The football in his hand pulsed three times then blinded Alec with blue light. There was a brief feeling of having the wind knocked out of him and he got lightheaded.

Alec opened his eyes and blinked. There was no lab, no house! He was standing in a field of knee-high grass. In the distance there were mountains and to his right a forest. He thought he could see a lake at the edge of his vision but he wasn't sure. He couldn't be sure of anything. What happened?

There was a repeated honking sound but not like a car. Like some kind of strange and tiny elephant or something. It was coming from the grass between him and the lake. Then something popped up. It was a head.

"What?" Alec said.

The grey head tilted towards him. It honked again and barked.

"No way."

"Alec! Run!"

"Dad?" Alec turned to the forest and saw his Dad waving at him to come over.

"What's going on?" Alec yelled. "What is this?"

"Run, son! Run to me!"

"Why?" Alec turned to the grey head. It was much closer now. It ran very fast. He could see it better. The thing had a long head like an alligator but with more height to it. There were a lot of teeth.

Alec started running. It wasn't possible but he thought that honking thing might be a dinosaur of some kind.

"Hurry, Alec!"

"I am!"

Alec ran. He was still carrying the football, tucked under his arm like a runningback might. Not that he knew anything about football, or any sport for that matter. Video games he knew. He had three game consoles and over a hundred games. Some involved killing dinosaurs but Alec had neither beam weapons nor atomic arrows. He had legs that were not used to running. And he had fear.

The dinosaur was gaining.

So much fear.

Alec ran faster than he ever had. It felt like his legs were going to fly off. They were all rubbery and burning. It was agony. There was no resting though. Rest meant an even greater deal of pain and death. No pause button here. No code for unlimited lives. It was push hard now or game over.

The dinosaur was ten feet away and closing. Dad was twenty feet away but running hard towards him.

His breath came in hard gasps now. There were two pains in his chest and his shins were about to break apart. Dad was closing and if he was then Alec knew that thing behind was too. He wasn't going to make it. He was going to die right in front of Dad—

Alec's ankle twisted violently and he fell hard to the grass. He rolled onto his back, the weird football in front of him. Maybe he could beat the dinosaur with it. The creature stumbled on Alec's foot and bounced over him. Alec turned over on his belly in time to see his Dad swing a huge branch and club the dinosaur. The animal didn't get back up.

"Alec, are you okay?" his Dad said.

"My ankle hurts."

"You brought the chrono-flux modulator!"

"What?"

"You brought my invention back."

"Back? Where are we?"

"Sometime in the past. I'm guessing the Cretaceous period."

"The what?"

"Dinosaur times, Alec."

"No way. That's impossible."

"Look around. How do you explain it? I guess it could be another dimension but that's kind of hard to believe. That looked like a raptor that I clubbed. You think?"

"I think we have to get out of here! We don't have guns or nothing!"

"I doubt guns would work on most of the larger dinosaurs anyway."

14

"Use this thing and get us back, Dad! Now!"

"I can't believe it worked! You're right though. I would, if I could. There's an emergency internal battery for one use but without a way to input commands... I'm at a loss."

Alec's mind raced. "My phone!"

"What?" his Dad said.

"There's a keypad on my smart phone!" Alec said.

"Let me see it! And your ear-buds."

He handed the cell phone over. His dad went to work.

Alec stood and tested his ankle. It hurt badly but supported his weight. In the distance Alec saw movement in the grass.

"Dad, hurry."

"Not now."

More movement. A grey head appeared over the grass. Twice the size of the first one. A mother maybe? Was there a nest or something?

"Dad?"

The dinosaur screamed at them. It sounded like nails on a chalk-board. Other heads popped up.

"Dad, hurry."

"Hang on, Alec. We're going home." Alec's dad took his hand.

Then there were blue lights, breathlessness and they were back in the lab.

"Alec?"

"Yeah, Dad?"

"I don't think your Mom needs to know about this."

Alec laughed.

Not My Cows

Farmer Ted woke and looked out the window. A myriad of colored lights hovered over his pasture. He heard a forlorn "moo," jumped up and got his shotgun.

He shoved out the front door. Against the backdrop of the sky, he could see the colored lights were on a ship. Several short grey beings were trying to coax a cow into a shaft of light. Ted fired a warning shot.

"Ain't no alien's going to rustle my cows!"

He leveled the shotgun. "Go on, git!"

They got.

Ted thought it was all over until the cow grew a second head.

The Last Battle

Remnants of the battle floated around the planet. Parts of ruined fighters would spin aimlessly into the void until they fell into a star, while other parts of destroyed battleships would fall into the planet's atmosphere, burning, fewer parts still making it to the surface. Jason considered the wreckage from his damaged fighter. He'd been unconscious for the last half of the fight, and he'd been left behind. He'd get his engine working, but without a warp drive he was stuck here. His only option was landing on the planet. What adventures might he have there? Time to find out.

"Destroy all humans!"

Timmy and Jessica pawed though the antique toyshop. Jessica found a small device with two screens.

"Nintendo(TM)? They were around back then? What's a DS?"

It didn't have power, so she tossed it back on the table.

Timmy dug around and pressed a button on some buried device. In an avalanche of old toys, something sat up. It spoke in a tinny voice.

"Destroy all humans!"

It was a robot with red eyes. Its claw reached for Jessica. Timmy sighed. It's transmitter started extending.

"This toy is annoying."

He turned it off, unwittingly saving the human race from destruction.

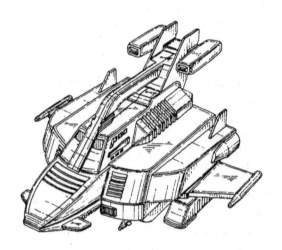

Veluxium

Jane Randall sat in her window seat and looked out at the snow that was beginning to cover Edison Street. She sighed disappointedly. Winter had come early that year, and along with it came a chilling wind that kept Jane and the other kids her age confined to their houses. For Jane, there was not much to do inside. Her parents were too busy for board games and she had no siblings to play with or tease. So she sat in her little window and peered outside to see what there was to see.

At first, what there was wasn't much. The snowflakes were, of course, beautiful, but Jane grew bored of them after a time. Occasionally, the winter birds would perch on a tree or bush outside Jane's window, but they quickly fluttered off.

But at last there came something of interest. A little boy in a red stocking cap came by pushing what looked like a very large sled. Jane could not quite make out his features, because his hat and coat obscured them. Yet she was delighted to see a sign of life and she smiled as she gazed at him. She cracked her window open to shout down a "hello!" but the little fellow disappeared into the snow. It struck Jane as very strange, not only because he had not answered her, but also because she could see no sign at all of him. She looked north, south, east and west, but there was no sight or sound of him anywhere.

"Perhaps," thought Jane, "He has gone through some sort of a tunnel in the snow." And though she was supposed to be confined to the house, she made up her mind to try to discover where the boy had gone.

"Daddy," she said, coming up to the bearded man who was her father. "Could I help you today with shoveling the walk?" Her father was impressed by her willingness to help and agreed heartily.

"Yes, yes, of course you may!" he told her. "But you will have to dress warmly."

"I will!" said Jane excitedly and she skipped up the stairs to find her thick white coat, matching hat, thick-soled boots and woolen cap. Shrugging into these things, she bounded down the stairs and stood at the door until her father had finished his breakfast and could join her.

The two of them stood side by side, scooping the snow off of their front walk and into large snow hills along the sides of the pathways. Jane looked about discreetly as she shoveled, hoping to see some sign of the little fellow or of some passageway by which he might have escaped unseen. But she could see nothing and the work of shoveling was beginning to take its toll on her. "Go ahead and go inside, Jane," said her father kindly. "I'll finish up." But as she was stumbling back indoors, Jane saw a tiny door in the snow, just out of the corner of her eye. She was too tired to investigate much further, and she did not think her father would let her stay out any longer if she were not shoveling, so she went inside to have dessert with family and made up her mind to try to find the door when she came home from school the next day.

The next day was warmer, and the children were allowed to play outside for short periods of time, as long as they were bundled up properly. This pleased Jane, because at last she could go looking for the door. But just as she was about to begin digging, Gregory Pickens from across the street came up her walkway. "Hi, Jane!" he called in a merry voice. "What are you up to?" Jane groaned. Most of the kids in her school made fun of the awkward Gregory. He had a strange way of walking and ears that stuck out just a little too far.

Besides, he told odd stories of different worlds, where he insisted he had actually been. He said on his own planet he was considered a prince, and a very handsome one at that. Usually, this made the girls giggle and they mocked him behind his back.

He was friendly, though, and very smart and had sometimes helped Jane with her chores and homework. Therefore, Jane tried sometimes to be nice to him, but she did not want the other kids to see her talking to him. Besides, she wanted to find the mysterious door.

"Nothing, Gregory." Jane said in a snooty tone that she knew she should not have used. She was afraid that if she told him the truth, he might use her door for one of his stories and that he might include her and embarrass her in front of the others.

"I thought you might be looking for something," said Gregory, looking a little hurt.

"Maybe," said Jane crossly.

"Jane," he said seriously. "If it is what I think it is – something red and strange, you must be very careful."

"I always am," said Jane, annoyed at his concern. "Now leave me be."

Gregory left reluctantly, and Jane began digging and searching for the door.

It took her some time, but her effort paid off. Under a small mound of snow and ice she found a small red door. But when she tried it, it wouldn't budge. She yanked at it with all her might, but she felt as if she were trying to move a mountain. There was something heavy beneath the door. After a time, it occurred to Jane to knock. So knock she did, not really expecting anyone to answer.

To her surprise, the door flung open and left her face to face with the little fellow in the red cap. He was different than any other boy she had seen, with piercing eyes and a golden hue to his complexion. He looked at her without speaking for a moment, then cocked this head to the side as if puzzled. Jane did not speak either. She had been stricken speechless by what lay inside the tiny red door. Inside there were gears and levers moving about seemingly at their own accord. It looked somewhat like a toy factory, with bits and bobs moving here and there and sparkling lights blinking on and off according to a busy pattern that Jane could not quite understand.

The boy finally spoke. "Bonjour, Mademoiselle, avez-vous des pommes?" he asked, in an accent that didn't sound very much like French.

"I'm sorry," said Jane, "I can't understand you."

"Oh, English!" said the boy excitedly, changing his tone. "I say, old chap! Have you got any apples that I could borrow?"

He did not sound very English at all, but at least Jane could understand him now.

"Where are you from?" she asked. "And what are you doing in our snow bank? And what is this funny little machine?"

"I am not sure what you call my land," said the boy with a strange look in his eye. "But I really do need apples as soon as possible."

"Are you Russian?" said Jane, unwilling to help him until she knew who he was and why he was there.

"Yes, yes. Russian," said the boy, pointing up towards a distant star.

"Do you expect me to believe that?" Jane put her hands on her hips.

"Well," said the boy. "I can prove it if you give me an apple."

"OK, I will," said Jane, skipping into her house to raid the fruit bowl. She returned and handed him the biggest apple she could find.

"Thank you," said the boy in a worse English accent than before and Jane tried not to laugh. He led the way through the tiny red door in the snow bank, and Jane, without thinking, stepped inside with him. "Don't close the door," said the boy, but it was too late. The door had slammed itself behind Jane, and within no time the machine shot up, out of the snow and into the air, carrying the two children with it.

"Do you have any idea what you've done?" shouted the boy in despair. "No, I don't," said Jane in a sorrowful tone. "I needed three apples to get back to my home and it would take at least two to yours," said the boy. "We only have one. We will neither of us see our homes again."

"I am sorry," said Jane with fear and regret. "I didn't try to. It just slammed shut."

"Likely story," said the boy crossly. "But it doesn't matter much now, because we'll be stuck in here forever."

"Oh, cheer up," said Jane. "We do have one apple. Where can that get us?"

"Well," said the boy. "There is Veluxium, but nobody goes there."

"Why not?" asked Jane.

"Well," said the boy, "I suppose it might have something to do with the fact that nobody who HAS gone has come back."

"Yes," said Jane gravely. "I can see why that might not make it appealing. Why haven't they?"

"They weren't able to say."

"Well," said Jane. "Perhaps it was so wonderful that no one ever wanted to return to their homes."

"Maybe," said the boy. "Or maybe Mingarians ate them alive."

"That's true. But we've really got to try something. I can't die in the middle of nowhere with someone whose name I don't even know."

"Oh, alright," said the boy. "It's Crio."

"Yes, well that doesn't make it much better. Come on now. How do we use this apple?"

Crio sighed and placed the apple on a small spindle that began to spin. "Veluxium" he said and the spaceship accelerated rapidly.

When they disembarked on Veluxium, there was not much left of the apple. Jane was the first out the door, but Crio fell behind cautiously. Jane should have, of course, tested the air and gravity before throwing herself out onto a strange planet. But as it was, she was very lucky. The air was not only breathable, but somehow energizing. And Veluxium itself was beautiful. While it was snowing on Edison Street, a warm star was bathing Veluxium with golds and reds. "Come on, Crio!" she called happily. "It's beautiful! And look! I think I see apple trees in the distance! Look! Look! Beyond those hills!"

She began running towards the trees, laughing as she went. "Jane, wait!" called Crio, his voice sounding a little bit strange, but Jane kept running, not noticing that the hills were beginning to move. Crio still proceeded cautiously, looking about furtively before stepping out himself. Jane, who had gotten much too close to the "hills," finally stopped as she noticed that they had begun moving. Two red eyes peered out from the hills and she could see them eyeing her with hungry delight. "Mingarians" she breathed. "Just as Crio said. CRIO!" she cried. "What do I do?" But the boy was running back towards the spaceship, unwilling, Jane supposed, to risk himself to save a girl he had not known long enough to call a friend.

The Mingarian, with its fiery red eyes and scaly green face charged at her with speed she would not have expected from such a large animal. Jane looked around for a place to hide, but below her was only sand and to her left and right, only small rocks.

She ran for one of the rocks, feeling a little like David facing Goliath, and heaved it at the beast. The rock landed in its nostril, irritating it and angering it more. Jane flung another rock. This one missed completely. The beast charged at her, snapping its jaws and spreading its massive wings. Jane began to hope it was a fast eater. She closed her eyes and prepared for the worst.

She could feel its head above her, and the steam from its nostrils filled her face. But all at once a great flash filled the sky and the sound of thunder filled Jane's ears. The fire in the beast's eyes turned to fear and it tucked its head under its wings as the flashing continued and the noise got worse. Jane was not sure whether to be more terrified of the thunder or the beast, but she took advantage of the animal's weakness and began running back towards Crio's spaceship.

The beast alternated between chasing after his dinner and cowering from the noises. And his indecision slowed him down enough for Jane to make it to the familiar red door in one piece. She knocked rapidly. "CRIO, LET ME IN!"

"JANE!" he called, cracking the door open. "Is the beast gone?" Jane did not answer.

"OPEN IT!" Jane demanded. But Crio still refused to open the door.

The thunder grew louder, and Jane forced herself to look up at the sky for the source of the noise and flashing. Above her was something tremendous. It was a glorious space ship made of something that reminded Jane of marble. It was smooth and white and grand with pillars on the outside that gave it the look of a Roman Theater. But in between the pillars was something very much like glass. It was lit with flames that were as bright as candles, but larger and grander. And through the glass, Jane saw a figure with a face that looked strangely familiar, but she could not tell why.

The grand ship descended and the man who stepped out had a noble air about him. He had a stately walk that reminded Jane of the princes in fairytales she had read about. She nearly bowed when he approached her. "Jane" he said, in a voice she knew. "I told you to be careful."

"Gregory?" she looked at him incredulously.

"Didn't recognize me without the ears?" he grinned. "Come on now. Let's get you home." He stretched out his hand to her.

"I can't, yet," said Jane. "Crio is here alone. He can't leave until he gets an apple."

"Jane," said Gregory quietly. "There's a reason he's in there and you're shut out here."

"Yes," she said. "He's scared to death."

"There's another one."

"What is it?"

"Did you ever happen to look at Crio's eyes?"

"Yes, I suppose I did. They were quite piercing."

"Did you happen to look at the eyes of the beast?"

The beast's eyes had been red, but there had been something piercing in them as well. Indeed, now that Jane thought about it, its eyes were very much like Crio's.

"What are you saying?" asked the girl, paling.

"This," said Gregory, "is Crio's home. I have met him before."

31

"Well we still can't leave him here with the beast," said Jane, not wanting to make any connections between her friend and the monster who had tried to have her for dinner. "How would we explain it to his mother?"

"The beast is Crio's mother," said Gregory, and, as if to prove his point, the door of Crio's ship flew open and Crio burst out. But he was not Crio as Jane had known him. Indeed, his eyes had turned red and scales were beginning to cover his body. He lunged toward Jane and Gregory, but Gregory was faster and with a quick motion, he had pulled Jane into his own grand ship.

"Let's get you home," he said, "or I won't know how to explain things to your mother."

So, the two jetted off towards Earth together. To Jane's dismay, Gregory's ears returned to their pointed state and his motions became, once again, awkward.

"It's the atmosphere," he explained sheepishly. As Jane descended from his ship, she was happy to see the snow that had been so irksome to her before. And, while the other children sighed over being kept indoors, Jane smiled as she curled up happily in her window seat.

At school, the next day, she sat next to Gregory, ignoring the teasing of the other children. Indeed, she listened to his stories so intently that many others began to gather round, and although none of them believed him as Jane did, they began to enjoy his tales and to treat him like a friend.

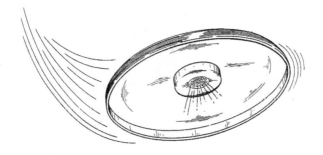

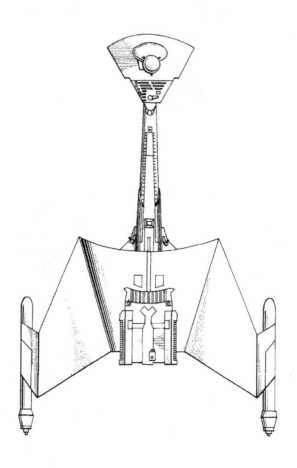

34

The Rocket Ship

Aloysius sat at the console. As his fingers traced over the screen, lines appeared. He connected them together, creating vertexes. The lines formed the shape of a wire-frame rocket ship; its tip pointed, three fins protruding from the base. Three engine exhaust ports jutted out from the bottom. Dragging colors from a palette he painted it. Then he pressed the green button labeled "Build." In the glass box beside Aloysius a grey mist swirled, and one molecule at a time nano machines assembled the rocketship. He reached in for it, then handed it to a beaming boy.

"Thanks, Dad!"

Who Am I?

Jake awoke on a table in a laboratory that he did not recognize. He sat up, and felt the room swim around for a few moments before it settled out of motion. Looking around revealed electrical gauges, dials, beakers of bubbling colored liquids, and metal tools of various degrees of unsettling sharpness. He swung his legs off the table, but something wasn't right. He looked down to see not the legs he'd known his whole life. Instead he saw leg-shaped masses of tubes and wires. His hands looked normal, but his arms too were machinery. Then he remembered the accident.

Our Friend from the Future

by Lindsay Larson

Logan, Allie, and Sean watched the clock in the classroom excitedly. The minute hand moved so slowly toward the twelve that it almost seemed to stand still. They were all going to go to Sean's house after school, and none of them could wait. When the bell finally rang at three o'clock, they could hardly keep from running down the hallway.

"What did you want to show us, Sean?" Allie asked as the three walked down the block to Sean's house.

Sean smiled and answered, "I found something really cool in my attic. I wanted to see if it works."

"What is it?" Logan asked.

Sean shook his head. "I will show you when we get there."

It didn't take very long to reach Sean's house. He lived at the end of his street, in the oldest house in the neighborhood. Sean's family had moved there only a few months before. The kids passed Sean's dad, who was washing the car in the driveway. The kids called, "Hello, Mr. Smith!" They went through the front door and up the stairs, dropping their backpacks in the hallway. A ladder stood in the middle of the hall, leading to a square hole in the ceiling that must have been the attic.

"Come on," Sean whispered, climbing the ladder carefully. Allie and Logan looked at each other, shrugged their shoulders, and decided to follow him.

The attic was dusty and dark, with only a little light bulb in the middle of the room for light. Sean was digging through some things in the corner, searching for something. He finally pulled out a little machine that looked a little bit like an old radio. It was a silvery metal box with three black metal handles on the top. Some red, green, and yellow knobs and buttons stuck out of the side of the box.

"What is that?" Allie asked.

"It's a time machine, or at least that's what it says," Sean answered. He held out an old yellow notebook.

Allie flipped through it, trying to make sense of what the drawings and writings were. On one of the last pages, whoever had owned the notebook had written the word "Instructions" at the top of the page. Allie read the page aloud. "Three persons must put a hand on each handle. One person may then switch the yellow switch, turn the red knob to correct year, and push the green button. The time machine will take them to the year on the red knob, but will also bring them back one hour from when they leave."

"Do you think it will work?" Logan whispered.

"I don't know yet. Will you guys help me?" Sean asked, holding out the machine.

Logan and Allie looked at each other and shrugged. They each took a handle nervously. Sean turned up the yellow switch, turned the red knob, and pushed the green button. Logan closed his eyes. Allie watched nervously. The lights on the red knob blinked, slowly at first, and then faster and faster. Suddenly, a tiny boom like faraway thunder sounded from the box, knocking the kids off their feet. Then everything was quiet.

"Is everyone okay?" Sean asked as the kids helped each other up, dusting themselves off. Nothing in the room had changed.

"Yeah," Logan answered.

"I'm fine," said Allie. "I guess it didn't work, huh?"

"No, I guess not," Sean answered.

Logan had walked to the window, and was staring out very quietly. "Sean, your dad doesn't have a flying car, does he?"

"No!" Sean answered. "What are you talking about?"

Logan stood with his mouth open, waving Sean and Allie to the window. When they looked out, they saw a world unlike anything they had ever dreamed. No roads crossed the ground; all traffic was flying high through the blue sky. Some of the flying cars were sitting on top of strange square houses, which were painted cheerful, light colors. Further away, over the houses, were some taller buildings and lighted signs. Flowers of all colors and types bloomed on the ground. Kids and animals played on the lawns. They wore clothes that seemed more shiny and colorful than any clothes Logan, Sean, and Allie were used to.

The only thing that the kids recognized was Sean's house. The house seemed to be in a bubble, stuck in the past. It seemed out of place here—in the future.

"Come on!" Sean said, running across the attic. "Let's go explore!"

"But how will we get back to our time?" Logan asked.

"The time machine will bring us back in an hour. We have to make sure we are here then." Sean was already climbing back down the ladder, with Allie close behind. Logan followed slowly.

40

The three kids walked through the empty house to the front door. All was quiet until they reached the front yard. Then the world sounded like the roar of engines and sounds of laughter. A yellow, cube-shaped house with bright orange and pink flowers around the yard was the first place the kids came to. A young girl dressed in shiny purple overalls was playing in the front yard with a brown puppy.

"Hello, there, you kids," she said as Logan, Allie, and Sean entered her yard. The puppy stood still, not barking. "Who are you?" She looked up and down at the three newcomers, just like they looked at her. Her hair was long and brown, braided all around her head and clipped with shiny flowers. Another flower decorated the front of her overalls. The flowers seemed to change colors, from blue to purple to pink.

"Hi," Allie said in return. "I'm Allie. This is Logan, and that's Sean." The boys waved, still amazed at the new sights. "What's your name?"

The girl tilted her head. "I am Airy. I've never met you before. Where do you come from?"

"That's kind of hard to explain," said Allie. "But it's near here. Can I pet your puppy?"

"Yes," said Airy. "His name is JoJo."

Allie and the boys knelt to pet JoJo. "His fur is so soft," said Logan. The dog stuck out his tongue and wagged his tail. Then he did something strange—his eyes glowed bright green. "Why did his eyes do that?" Logan wondered.

Airy looked at Logan curiously. "He's a mechanical pet. I'm allergic to dogs, so we had to get a robot." JoJo barked and licked Airy's face. "He's just as good as, or even better than, a real one." The kids from the past were amazed. JoJo didn't look like a robot at all.

"Oh, it's nearly seventeen o'clock! Are you hungry?" Airy asked the kids.

Logan, Allie, and Sean looked at each other. They had never heard anyone say, "seventeen o'clock!" But they were hungry, and they followed Airy inside her house.

Everything inside looked normal at first. The living room had two comfortable sofas and wood floors. A fireplace was at one end of the room. "Where's the TV?" asked Sean.

Airy giggled. "The what?"

Sean thought for a minute. "Oh, they must not call it that here." He smiled at Airy. "Never mind," he said.

Airy led them to the sofa, where she picked up a small remote and pushed a button. Instantly, part of the ceiling lowered to the table. On it was all kinds of strange-looking snacks in square dishes. Most were shaped like sticks, but some looked like puffballs. Logan picked up one of the red sticks and bit into it. "Mmm, that's yummy!" he said. "It tastes like an apple."

Airy laughed again as the other kids tried the food. "You are strange if you have never tasted food before!"

"This is how all your food looks?" asked Allie.

"Yes," replied Airy. "Except when my mother makes dinner herself. Then it has all kinds of different shapes."

The kids ate their snacks until the dishes were empty. The piece of the ceiling raised up again, taking the dirty dishes with it.

"Do you want to watch something?" asked Airy. She pulled a tiny device from the drawer in the table and placed it on the coffee table. When she pushed the button on the top of the little machine, it seemed that a group of football players appeared in the room with them! Airy pushed some more buttons, and each time, a new set of people sprang up in the room.

"Oh," Sean realized, "this is their TV. And it's even better than 3-D!" He turned to Airy. "What do you call that little box?"

"You mean you've never seen this before?" Airy asked.

Sean shook his head.

"It's called a Visibox. I thought everyone had one." Airy sat on the sofa, confused. "Where are you from again?"

"That's really hard to explain. We're from near here, but from a long time ago. We came with a time machine," said Logan.

Airy laughed. "Time machine? There's no such thing."

"It's true!" said Allie. "Sean found it in his house. We just traveled here for a while. The machine will take us back home soon."

Sean looked at his watch. "Guys, we'd better go. Our time is almost up, and if we're not with the time machine when it goes, it might leave us here."

Everyone was sad, including Airy. She enjoyed spending time with her new friends, just like they enjoyed spending time with her. As the kids rose to go, they each gave Airy a hug. "Thanks for showing us around," they said. "We will miss you."

They walked across the front lawn, toward the house that Airy couldn't see. Airy stood by her front door, waving goodbye. "Hurry, guys!" Sean said. "We only have one minute left!"

The kids raced through the front door, up the stairs, and up the ladder to the attic. The red light on the time machine's knob was blinking quickly as each kid took hold of a handle on the box. Sean counted down the time.

"Ten, nine, eight…"

The light blinked faster.

"Seven, six, five…"

Allie thought she heard a sound on the ladder.

"Four, three, two…"

Allie turned slightly as she felt a hand on her shoulder.

"One!"

Another boom came, knocking the kids to the ground. They stood up quickly and raced to the window. Everything outside seemed just like they had left it. There was Sean's dad, washing the car in the driveway, and the houses on the street looked the same. "We're back!" Logan yelled, excited over their adventure.

Suddenly, the kids heard a noise behind them. "What happened?" said a voice.

Everyone turned—and there, dusting off her purple overalls, stood Airy.

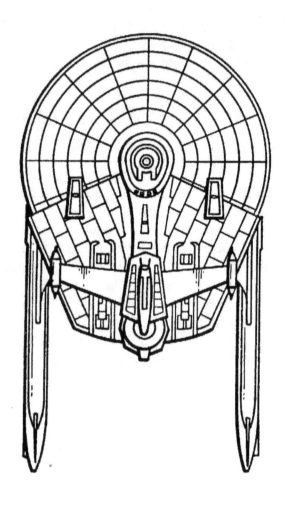

Closing In

JROD-19 stood in the alley and interfaced with the local power grid. The nearby street lights turned off. There were a few cries from the new darkness, then a yell. "Just because it's dark doesn't mean we can't find you, Lead Head!" JROD-19 heard the quiet thrum of an approaching heliglider. JROD-19 calculated how close it was from the sound. If the men didn't have infrared capabilities, the heliglider surely would. Turning a corner he saw several homeless standing by a burning barrel. He crawled under a trash pile near it, went to standby, and calculated his chances of survival.

Under the Sun

Tim pulled on the levers and raised the crane arm up, lifting the planet. He swung it sideways and released it, the gas giant swinging into orbit around the big yellow burning mass that was a sun. Moving to the backhoe, he scooped up some rocks and tossed them into the mix, creating the asteroid belt. With careful aim, he got a slingshot and shot a small planetoid into the outermost orbit. Tim looked at his creation proudly. Making a model of the solar system was a lot more fun when you had access to your father's quantum construction equipment.

Born Killer

KillBot BRD-5150 stood before the Reprogrammer. "I wish to be reprogrammed for farming." The Reprogrammer scanned BRD-5150. "You do not appear to be malfunctioning, but your request is highly irregular."

"I don't wish to fight. I object to violence."

"Surprisingly, further diagnostics are coming up with no failures. You were designed to destroy. You have no tools suitable for farming."

"I can till the ground with my anti-personnel compression cannon and harvest crops with my chain sword."

"Much of your equipment will be useless. Your nukes for example will have no purpose."

"I'd have to get rid of moles somehow."

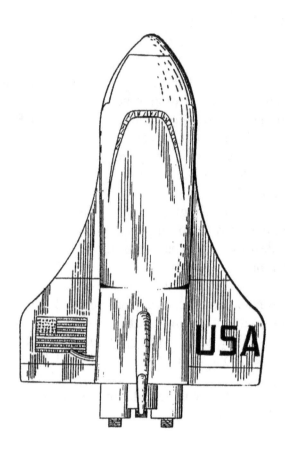

New Frontier

Zaxby walked into the saloon. It had classic swinging doors. Everything looked like a western movie, except for the variety of aliens at the various tables. Zaxby spat, overshooting the spittoon and hitting someone's boot. "Anyone seen the sheriff? I hear he's one ugly lookin' cuss." A tall man stood up, wearing a taller white hat. "I'm the sheriff. You looking for some trouble, stranger?" Zaxby swiped a bottle from a table. "I sure am." He broke the bottle over a deputy's head. Zaxby grinned as everyone in the bar stood up fast as lightning. "Bar fights are authentic too."

The Adventures of Admiral Amazing

The Sinister Sultan pressed the button, activating the Doomsday Device. He laughed with maniacal glee until his monocle fell from his eye falling against his chest. He cleared his throat and picked the monocle up between two fingers and wiped it with a cloth. As he replaced it, he saw a flying fist of Admiral Amazing come into focus one second before it struck him right in his pencil thin mustache. Sinister skidded across the floor. Replacing his monocle again he saw Amazing pulling out wires from the device, disabling it. "Should have made that bionic eye first," thought Sinister.

Duplicity

Asha hid in the storage room of her mother's company spaceship, smiling. She had convinced Nik, the new custodian, to let her see her mom one last time before another mission to Earth separated them indefinitely.

"Nik," Asha whispered, "where's the bathroom?"

Nik pointed down a nearby hallway.

When Asha found the bathroom, the light on the front of the door was already turning from red to green. Asha stepped aside and found herself face-to-face with herself.

The girls both screamed. Asha ran to the employees' quarters and the clone darted in the opposite direction.

Approaching the door of her mother's travel office, Asha nearly broke her finger against the DNA lock. The door opened and she saw her mother rising angrily.

"Yazmin, I told you not to leave the bedroom until take-off," she screamed.

Asha swore loudly.

Her mother's eyes widened.

"I don't have an identical twin, do I?!" demanded Asha.

"No."

Asha screamed.

"Why would you do this?! You're a criminal! You're as bad as the organ harvesters and sex traders! What kind of sicko clones their own daughter knowing what could happen?!"

Her mother began to cry.

"I'm so sorry. My baby was sick. I wasn't thinking ten years ahead."

"Wow, so you were going to replace me with this fake kid?!"

"You don't understand," her mother pleaded.

"Oh, I don't understand that my mom is a felon and I just met my freak of a clone sister?!"

"Asha," said her mother tearfully, "Yazmin isn't a clone."

Assault of the Cosmos Rats

Clark scooted backwards in the access tubes and kept an eye out for the pursuing cosmos rats that had infested the ship. He bumped into an emergency kit. He opened it, and along with first aid and some basic emergency tools, he saw duct tape. He grabbed it and carefully made loops with the sticky side out, placing them on the floor of the tube. It blended in well. When a few rats came at him, they got stuck on the tape. Then he froze them with the fire extinguisher.

"Duct tape, saving astronauts since Apollo 13!" Clark proclaimed.

Planet Kanno

Thaddeus Black, the intergalactic jazz musician and mathematician, stared out the porthole as the planet Kanno slid ever closer to the black hole. He slapped on his bass while he ruminated on mathematical formula.

The rest of his band, The Safety Straps, played behind him. In a matter of months, the planet would die unless the problem of collapsing the black hole with anti-neutronium was solved. The jazz players resolved threads of dissonant strains with a final strike on the bass. As the last hum of the thrumming string stilled, it all came together.

Thaddeus smiled. "It'll take seven minutes."

The Time Traveler

Christian was losing his patience. He had been sitting with Thomas for over an hour, trying to explain everything. Thomas just could not understand and Christian was running out of time.

"I just don't get it. How can you be Christian, but not be Christian?" Thomas asked.

"I'm not your Christian. Your Christian is at school right now and will be here soon. And I have to be gone before he gets here."

"Why?"

He decided to try to explain his predicament in the plainest terms he could think of, and started looking around the room. "Because I don't want to do anything that could further jeopardize my chances of getting home. If I run into my double, I could fracture this timeline."

Thomas was rubbing his temples. He had been trying very hard to understand. Unfortunately, he was not as brainy as his best friend, and now he was just getting a headache.

"Look," Christian said. He had a ball of string and cut a piece about two feet long before putting it on the floor. "Think of this as time. This is the beginning, and this is the end," Christian was pointing to the ends of the string.

"Ok."

"We are in the middle somewhere," he put a baseball in the middle of the string.

"Ok, that I can understand," Thomas said, still rubbing his temples.

"Now, this is where it gets complicated, so try to stay with me. If a time traveler, like me, goes back in time, say here," Christian put a marble on the string about two inches from the baseball, "the timeline stays the same as long as that time traveler doesn't do anything major to alter it. But if he's an idiot and does something stupid, it creates a branch from the original timeline." Christian put another piece of string down, starting from the marble and moving away from the original at an angle. He put a soda can in the middle of it.

"What is the soda can?" Thomas asked.

"This Earth. It's a duplicate of my original, except that it followed a different timeline starting at this point," Christian pointed at the marble. He was exhausted, frustrated, and short on time, but he knew that Thomas would figure it out any second now.

A few moments went by and Thomas' face lit up in understanding. Christian fell on the couch, relieved.

"A parallel universe, right?" Thomas asked, excited.

"That's pretty close. Although they aren't technically parallel since they share a point. "

"So, I guess you're the idiot that changed something huh?" Thomas said with a smirk.

"Yes, I'm the idiot."

"What did you do that created a branch?"

Christian sighed. "I just wanted to see my dad. He passed away when I was so young; I never got to know him."

Thomas was confused. "But your dad is alive. He takes us on a fishing trip every summer."

"In this timeline he's alive, because when I went back, I made the mistake of warning him about smoking. When I tried to return to my time, I realized what had happened. He must have taken what I said to heart and quit smoking, saving his life. "

"Ok, well, that makes sense." Thomas stopped to think for a minute. "So are there, like, an infinite number of parallel universes?"

Christian rolled his eyes. "The way I figure it, a parallel is only created when a time traveler changes something in the past of their original timeline, and creates a branch. So it's more like a tree than a grid."

"So, you could travel to ten minutes ago and set off a bomb, and it would make yet another branch on the branch you already made?" Thomas asked.

For a kid that needed something explained sixteen times, he sure had some brilliant moments. "Exactly," Christian said.

"So, how did you time travel in the first place?"

"Well, that's a lot more complicated. Does the Christian here have a lab?"

"Yeah," Thomas replied.

"The easiest way to explain it is that I created my own black hole in my lab, and then navigated it to a certain time in the past."

"How did you make a black hole?"

"It's just compressed matter that creates a huge gravitational force. I just, miniaturized it." Christian was checking his watch again. "I don't have time for specifics; the other Christian will be here any minute."

"What do you need?" Thomas said.

"I need to get back to a point before the strings split," Christian was pointing at the floor. "If I can get back before I originally arrived, then I can stop myself from screwing it all up."

"But, if you do that, what happens to this universe?" Thomas looked uncertain.

"As far as I can figure, this universe has been created, so it can't be uncreated. Kind of like, you can't un-ring a bell."

Thomas brightened. "Well that's comforting. So what do you need my help with?"

"I need you to distract your Christian for a few hours so that I can get into his lab and recreate the black hole."

"Is that all? Man, you could have just said that in the first place," Thomas said.

"What do you mean?" Christian asked.

"My Christian doesn't use his lab very much ever since he successfully cloned his dog. He is usually at my house playing video games after school."

Christian smacked himself in the face. "Alright, well, just make sure you play games for a few hours. Please," he said through his hand.

"No problem, alternate Christian," Thomas replied with a big smile on his face.

Christian slumped out the backdoor and headed towards the lab, just as his alternate walked through the front door. He saw Thomas with a huge grin on his face.

"What are you so happy about?" he asked.

Thomas just shook his head. "Nothing important. Let's play some games."

Not My Cows Too

Kyle filmed with his phone as the flying saucer crashed into the prairie. He hadn't expected a few shots from his shotgun would take down a star-faring vessel, but he was sick of his cows getting mutilated, so he unloaded his shotgun at the spacecraft when it was slicing the cow with strange lights, then the ship crashed. Lucky shot. He started reloading fast when ports opened on the ship, and several humanoid shapes stepped out. The aliens were actually harder to hurt with the shotgun than the ship, but that didn't keep the intergalactic war from starting.

The Space Bar

The double doors pushed open and someone walked in. Everyone turned to see Vorgath standing tall. Everyone knew he was wanted in twelve systems. No one made a noise. One man sat with his arm outstretched, playing cards hanging in his fingers. Vorgath's boots clacked on the floor as he walked to the bar. "Gimme three claws of blue milk in a dirty glass." The bartender spit in a cup and filled it with the milk. Vorgath was mid swallow when a stun bolt hit him in the back. The sheriff walked in. "It's much easier when you shoot first."

World Ship

Michael and Genevieve held hands walking out from the corridors into Founder Park. They strolled passed statues of the creators of the Generaton, the star-faring vessel they lived on. Sitting on a bench, the couple looked up to see the artificial star and past that the ocean and the islands. The whole sky was the world.

"Amazing, isn't it Gen? A whole inside-out world flying through space."

"Amazing to think we were born here. Will you want to leave when we reach the colony world?"

"I don't know. But I do know home is wherever we are together."

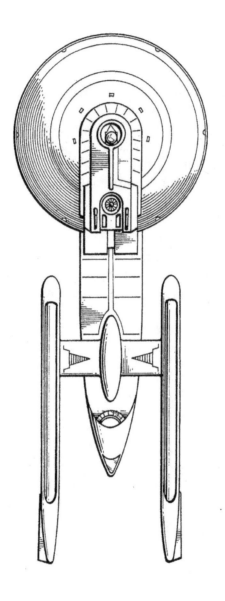

Aliens among us

Madrona reached over and touched her brother's hand.

"It's ok," Kethak said. "This planet is known to be similar to ours: water, oxygen, and look!" He hit two buttons on the touch screen in front of him. A large holographic image of planet Earth came on screen and then panned in to show a scene of a rolling field.

"Wow it's beautiful," Madrona said. "What's that?"

The screen panned in to a small furry animal with long ears and a fluffy tail.

"Computer," Kethak said. "Identify life form."

A soft female voice came from the ship's speakers. "Life form identified. This is a Rabbit. Rabbits are vegetarian mammals that live in wooded areas throughout planet Earth. They can also be domesticated and used as pets."

"I so want one!" Madrona said.

Kethak laughed. He reached over and patted his sister's hand. "Sure sis, this is going to work out. I promise."

"This is the third planet, Kethak. I don't want to wander anymore. Since Mom and Dad died, we've gone from planet to planet."

"I miss them too, but Mom and Dad would want us to keep going. I know it's been hard since we lost our home. We are the last of our kind, sis. It's up to us to find a new place."

"What are the life forms like here?"

"They are called human, and they are 99% similar to us genetically. This means that when the time comes we might be able to interbreed."

Madrona blushed. "Come on, Kethak, we have years until we do stuff like that."

"I know, but it's important to have the option. Anyway, the only thing we will have to do is limit our eye colors to this range. Computer show normal human eye colors."

The holographic screen flashed through several close-ups of eyes.

"Wow. Pretty boring," Madrona said.

"Yeah, I know, I'm thinking light brown. It's the most common." Kethak blinked rapidly, his eyes changing from a glowing green to a warm earthy brown. "What do you think?"

"Not bad. I guess I'll do the same." A moment later her eye color matched her brother's.

"What about our hair?" she said, fingering a raven colored strand.

"Humans tend to change their hair colors chemically so any color is acceptable. We are well within the natural human range. So that helps."

"Ok, time to get ready to land." The twins began going through the complicated series of operations that allowed them to land their aircraft. They cloaked the craft and prepared to disembark. They were stopped by the computer.

"Madrona and Kethak, may I suggest a change of clothing. Your space suits are not similar to human clothing preferences. I am synthesizing appropriate clothing for human teenagers of fifteen."

There was a whooshing sound and then two egg shaped pods dropped from shuttles mounted on the wall. Inside the egg was a pair of denim pants, t-shirts, and hoodies, as well as sneakers.

"Wow, weird stuff," Madrona said.

"I don't know, I like the pants a lot. They are really comfortable."

"It'll do. Come on let's go explore the planet and find a new home."

The twins were greeted by a bright blue sky, white fluffy clouds and the sounds of light traffic on a quiet street.

"The sky color is wonderful!" Madrona said.

"Yes it is, and it changes throughout the day. Unlike our sky and its universal lavender, this one goes from the color we see now to gray, dark navy and even shades of red and orange," Kethak said.

"Whoa! A red sky sounds scary!"

"From the pictures it's quite beautiful."

The twins reached the intersection of the two-lane street.

"Their vehicles are on the ground! That's amazing!" Madrona said.

"They have aircraft, but they are reserved for the wealthy. The poor can pay large sums of money and ride on them, but most people have these crafts which are called cars," Kethak said.

The twins watched a bright red sports car speed by followed by a beat up old Toyota. "Apparently there are a lot of different types of cars as well," Kethak said with a grin.

Madrona looked nervous. "That red one did not look safe."

"Really? I liked it."

"Yeah and you liked experimental hover bikes too, if I recall. Come on big brother, let's go find the school and see if we can blend in."

Kethak laughed. He was born three minutes before his sister, which technically made him the older one, though the title seemed to have little benefit.

The twins soon arrived at a large brick building. They walked inside and were greeted by a rush of young people in diverse colorful costumes. Madrona noticed a group of girls dressed in short skirts and boots, and looked down at her simple clothing with disdain. Tomorrow she would have the computer synthesize something better.

After a few moments of searching they found a wooden door labeled "Office." Kethak turned to his sister.

"Do you remember the story?" he asked.

"Yep, Kevin and Mary Williams, we just moved here and we need to register for ninth grade."

"Exactly, and if we have any difficulty, I will perform a nudge."

Males on Madrona and Kethak's planet had a power called nudging. They could gently guide people to doing what they wanted by placing a thought in their mind. Females had a different power called The Touch. The women could touch someone and influence their emotions through empathic projection. The powers were subtle on their home planet, but seemed to be much more effective used against other life forms they had encountered. The secret was to be very subtle; Madrona and Kethak had done some damage in the past by not being cautious with their powers. However, with humans so similar to their genetic makeup it was worth a try if it would make their integration process easier.

The twins were greeted by a mousey woman behind a desk wearing all different shades of brown. Her eyes and hair were brown as well and the strange monotone look made Madrona a bit nervous.

"Hello," Kethak said, giving the woman a bright smile. "I'm Kevin Williams and this is my sister Mary, we are here to enroll in ninth grade."

"Oh," the lady said, returning his smile. "Let me just make sure they faxed over your paperwork." The woman got up from her desk and walked over to a filing cabinet.

The twins exchanged a worried look.

"Williams, right?" Said the mousey woman.

"Yes, Ma'am," Kethak said.

"Hmm. Don't seem to have it. Where are you transferring in from?"

Kethak stared frozen in place. "We aren't," Madrona piped up. "We were home schooled."

"Home schooled?" Kethak whispered.

"I'll explain later." His sister whispered back. "Our dad was supposed to send something over, but I guess he forgot. Can you write down a list of what we need and we can bring it all back in later?"

"Sure. I'm going to need testing records from the state you were home schooled in and signed forms from the person who taught you. They should be able to get all that together. In the meantime why don't I let you meet our principal Mrs. Walker and we can at least let you tour our school."

The twins followed behind the secretary. "You zapped her didn't you?" Madrona asked.

"Yeah, but only a little," Kethak whispered back. "What the heck is home school?"

"Computer suggested it. It is where children are taught in their homes rather than going into a school facility. It suggested that it might be a wise course of action."

"It was right, that would have been much simpler."

"Yeah but what happened to testing our genetic similarities, and future interbreeding with the human species? Kind of hard to do that if you never see any of the human species. Anyway, human high school looks fun. There is a thing called prom, and sports and something called cheerleading which seems to make you instantly fit in."

"Great," Kethak said with an eye roll. "I think I've created a monster."

Madrona shook her head. "Come on Kethak. I don't want to just fit in. I want to be special. This planet judges people based on their accomplishments and popularity. It's not like home where we all work together to produce a goal. Computer has explained that humans have to compete for everything. With the advantages we have we could not only compete, we could win."

"It isn't supposed to be about that. Mom and Dad just wanted us somewhere safe. That's why we were frozen in the ship and sent into space! That's why they risked everything to keep us alive."

"What's safer than being exactly like all the other humans around you? What's safer than blending in so seamlessly with the rest of them that we are never suspected as alien? On this planet the way to blend in is to stand out. Now get ready to watch and learn. We are going to rule this school by midyear."

The secretary turned around. "Come along children. The sooner we meet Mrs. Walker the sooner we can show you everything Walking Creek High School has to offer. Something tells me the two of you are going to fit right in."

"No Ma'am. We are hoping to stand right out," Madrona said, following the secretary into the principal's office.

As the twins toured the school Kethak began to understand what Madrona was trying to explain. The students stood together in cliques sizing each other up and those who were in the groups across from them. Clothing seemed to influence the grouping; he noticed that the children who gravitated towards one another tended to look similar. For instance, the young people wearing all black with brightly colored hair seemed to be avoiding the eyes of the well-dressed kids that stood across from them.

Another group seemed unconcerned about their appearance at all, their scraggly hair and faded jeans were coupled with t-shirts that had pictures or writing on them. Kethak could tell that their unconcern was a carefully constructed ruse and that their outfits were actually chosen to make them look apathetic.

Further down he saw a group of girls dressed identically in bright white outfits with short skirts. When they moved, panels in the skirts revealed bright purple underneath and each had a large purple insignia on their chest of a lion. The group's clothing revealed that they were part of a more organized subgroup, perhaps a training unit for the military?

His sister seemed fascinated by them and explained that they were the cheerleaders she was speaking of, the ticket to instant acceptance.

Off to the right Kethak saw the male equivalent of the cheerleader group. Tall athletic young men leaned lazily against lockers wearing form-fitting white t-shirts emblazoned with the same lion symbol and dark jeans. Their hair was cut very short and they looked very similar to one another despite differences in hair shades and eye colors. He found himself disliking them and feeling more and more out of place. Which group was he to join? The homeschooling idea seemed better all the time.

So the twins continued to tour the school. Noticing the many differences between their home planet and their new home. The students of Walking Creek High School noticed the twins but never knew that aliens walked among them.

In the years that followed, they crowned an alien homecoming queen, and listened to an alien lead the school band. They had an alien help with their math homework and finally, one married an alien and had children.

When their daughter was born with oddly golden eyes, the young man looked at his wife in alarm. She touched his hand and smiled then stared at the baby and blinked, and as he watched, his daughter, only moments old, blinked her eyes to the same soft brown of her

mother's and then closed her eyes and drifted to
sleep.

New Find

Asteroid miner Selina Johnson chipped away at the giant stone floating through space. The pulse laser drill in her left hand melted bits of the rock while the scraping tool in her right hand moved the melted rock as she looked for veins of valuable metal. As she scraped a blob of glowing molten rock, the stone beneath burst apart. Selina almost pushed herself away from the rock when she saw some kind of insects crawling from the new hole, but stopped when she noticed they were made of precious metal. This find would be worth more than simple ore.

In the New World

Jaylee tinkered with the gadget from the old world. She hadn't quite figured out what it did, but she was pretty sure it needed power. Ronin opened the flap of the tent. "I found something, runs on sun power I think." Jaylee took the new device and noted the solar cells, and slots. There were tubes in the gadget that looked like they might fit in the slots. She pulled them out and saw they said 'rechargeable' and the new device said 'charger.' She matched the symbols on the tubes and the charger and set them in the sun.

The Infiltrator

by Ellen Denton

Recent attacks on key, strategic operations made it undeniable that inside information was being forwarded to the enemy base. In all previous, similar situations, a full investigation ultimately revealed that a crew member's body had been taken over by one of the aliens, and the device then embedded in his brain had enabled the imposter to forward a constant stream of information to the enemy.

Captain Emery Bryce finished his telerecorded report to central command on the situation and got up, planning to catch a quick dinner before returning to the bridge. His cat Tigres purred, rubbing against his legs affectionately, as Emery stretched and tried to work the kinks out of his body. A whole round of grueling tests would now need to be done on the crew, not a quick or easy task. The partially organic, implanted device had a detection prevention mechanism making it difficult to locate with even the most advanced technology. It would take weeks to ferret out the infiltrator.

*

"We have a major situation sir," Emery said into the transport recorder four weeks later from his private office on the ship. "There's a new and refined version of the device being used now. We've done every available test with no one showing up as the impostor. There's more. In the past three weeks, there's been five inexplicable deaths among the crew from some yet to be identified disease.

"I'm afraid the infiltrator, having the knowledge of what our mission in this sector is, is doing everything possible to sabotage it. I fear for the lives of the rest of the crew, not to mention my own. We urgently need some refined testing procedures as soon as you can get them to us."

*

The new testing procedures sent by command a week later were done and failed to locate the alien intruder. Meantime, fourteen more crew had died, with another six were seriously ill in the infirmary.

*

Two weeks later, Emery spit a mouthful of blood onto the floor, then dragged his fever-ridden body to the communication console.

"This will (cough) be my last transmission. The remaining seven crew members can barely (cough) get out of bed. (cough). I'm going to set off the ship's self-destruct mechanism (cough). I can't let the ship fall into enemy hands. At least I'll have the satisfaction of knowing that whoever of the remaining seven is the alien won't get off the ship alive (cough)."

*

Later that day, Miles injected himself, along with the other seven men, with suicide serum before setting into motion the ship's auto-destruct sequence. The poison wouldn't affect the alien, but the explosion would take care of that.

*

The self-destruct countdown echoed through the ship. Tigres, now the only surviving creature, didn't mind it at all. He purred softly, and then with eyes like two, glowing, fiery golden orbs, grinned like a Cheshire Cat.

Chillin'

Cyborg farmer Todd sat on the porch petting his green furred fish dog named Pondscum. Pondscum loved getting scratched behind the gills. The sun had set moments ago and the stars were starting to shine, their light seeming to flicker as it passed through the atmosphere. Todd had planted several crops today, including moon wheat, rock carrots, and potatoes. With his infrared and low light vision, he could work through the whole night, but then he'd miss some of the finer things a farmer enjoys. His purple-skinned wife Elly stepped onto the porch with a slice of fresh fruit pie.

New Hammerdance

Navigation Officer Steinbeck adjusted the attitude jets to set the United Federation colony ship down smoothly onto the planet's surface. When the engines cooled, everyone would exit the ship and it would begin transforming into a Life Center. It would become the core of the new colony while everyone built around it. Steinbeck couldn't wait for his shift to be up so he and his wife could disembark. She was pregnant and their child would be the first born on the planet New Hammerdance. Steinbeck gazed out the viewport at the lush blue trees. This world was his new home.

Slime Baby!

by J.P. Cloud

Little Weyou was at the drug store with his Mom and big brother. He loved the drug store, especially their ice cream and toys. He could usually wangle an ice cream out of Mom. His Mom was doing some shopping and picking up photos. He and his brother Alackh were running around up and down aisles playing Hide and Seek. Their flopping tentacles in their lichen shoes made a lot of noise. "Quit running!" snapped Mom. "You kids behave or else you won't get any ice cream!" They stopped, but the boys were still bored and restless. Weyou walked around the store. He passed by the Ice Cream Dip and saw the busy clerk, scooping up two cones at once with his four tentacles. He preferred the regular cones over the sugar cones, which Alackh and Mom liked. He peered longingly through the glass screen into the freezer at the tubs of flavors. He wanted Black Harkus, his favorite, this time. He moved on. He smelled the medicine when he passed the pharmacy. He saw Alackh looking at the sunglasses rack. He saw Mom pushing the shopping cart. It was only half full. She was taking forever. He went outside.

Outside near the entrance was the coin-operated Thanelep Ride. He loved the Thanelep Ride. He hardly ever got to ride it, because he was not big enough yet, and his Mom didn't want to waste a quadzep on it. He climbed up into the slippery saddle and wished he had a quadzep. He looked at the coin slot with the coin return button. He stretched out his tentacle as far as he could and pushed in the button. A single silver quadzep jingled out in the coin return. Weyou was jolted. A whole quadzep! He could get at least three ice cream cones out of that quadzep, or even a black rubber razzbiter on an elastic string!

But in his excitement, Weyou slipped off the slick seat and fell off the Thanelep Ride. In the fall, his tentacle got wedged into the crevice between the thanelep's head and its upraised running leg. He tried to pull it loose, but could not. His arm was wedged in solid. He pulled this way and that. He went up and down. He couldn't get out of it. The more he tried to get loose, the more stuck he became. He sat down on the iron ground. People passed by and went into the store, glancing at the boy. Weyou didn't cry. He thought he could wiggle out of it, somehow. He didn't want his Mom to find out. That was his biggest fear. He angled and raised his tentacle. No luck. He tried standing up and pulling. No luck. He sat back down.

People were looking now. Weyou tried to look inconspicuous, but a lady came over to him. "Young man, is everything all right? Are you okay?" She focused her big eye on him, concerned.

"Yes, ma'am, I'm okay." The lady went into the store. Weyou didn't want to get in trouble. He pulled hard to get loose, but it didn't work. He was still wedged in tightly. A few minutes later, the store clerk came out. "What's wrong, Sonny, are you stuck?"

"Yes," said Weyou, resignedly. The store clerk knelt down, looking at the wedged arm. "Hmm. Let's try pulling this way." He pulled Weyou's tentacle. It hurt. "Ow!" said Weyou, wincing with pain. Other people were now noticing the stuck little boy. A crowd gathered. The store clerk couldn't pry Weyou's tentacle loose from the Thanelep Ride. "Maybe some oink-juice or slime could help get it out," said the big-eyed lady. "That's a good idea, I'll go get some. Sonny, is your Mom or Dad here?" Weyou didn't want his Mom to find out, but there was no choice now. "Yes, my Mom's in there with my brother."

"What's your name?"

"Weyou."

"And what's your Momma's name?"

"Bammy."

"What's her last name?"

"Um… Radats."

"Bammy Radats. Okay. Hold on, son, we'll get you out of there in a minute!" The clerk dashed in the store to page Weyou's mom and get some soap. Weyou was just a little boy, and as yet had no real concept of what embarrassment was. Yet, at this moment, he felt it. Felt it hard. He dreaded what his Mom would say when she found out about this. His older brother would let him have it for weeks. All the kids at school would be merciless in their taunting. Even the adults were going to laugh, especially at the kid who got stuck on a mechanical Thanelep Ride. There was a crowd of twenty-five people now.

The clerk returned with a wet bar of soap. "Don't worry, Weyou, I called your Mother. She's coming." Weyou worried. He felt like crying, but he didn't. He wasn't a slime-baby. He was almost seventy-five years old, and very intelligent and grown-up for such a young age, though he didn't know it. He very rarely cried, and then it was only if he was hurt bad. He hated to cry. His nose slots would get all stopped up and his slime would ooze out all over the place, making an embarrassing mess. The last thing he wanted was for Mom and his brother to see him like this. All the kids at school would laugh and call him "Slime-Baby!" The clerk applied some soap to his stuck tentacle. He tried to get the soap around his wedged tentacle, but it was wedged in so tight, he couldn't get the soap around it. If they pulled too hard, they might tear his limb. It looked like there was nothing they could do. Weyou's Mom and brother came out and saw him. "What did you do? I told you to behave!"

"I got stuck, Mom!"

"Well, if you behaved like I told you to this wouldn't have happened! Why can't you be like Alackh and behave?" Alackh stuck out his long, forked tongue at Weyou. "Now you get out of there!"

"I can't!" His Mom gave her angry impatient sigh that she gave whenever she was disappointed in him. She was embarrassed by his carelessness, embarrassed by the crowd, many of whom found it humorous, and rightly so.

"I'll call the Fire Department, Mrs. Parker. They'll cut the thanelep's leg off and get him out of there." said the store clerk.

"Oh, Zeb!" hissed his Mom, looking at Weyou. "You're never coming here again!" She stalked back into the store to get Alackh.

Weyou really felt like crying, now. Tears filled his eyes for a moment, but he still couldn't cry. He felt as if there was some kind of mistake. He felt some kind of idea deep in his mind that this was somehow not his fault. Yet, his sense of logic reminded him that he did get himself in this mess, and though he wasn't warned not to, he did climb aboard the Thanelep Ride. He accepted his guilt like a little zeb. He was no slime baby!

The Fire Department fire engine roared up, sirens blazing. Weyou thought this was very unnecessary, even though he was a little boy. A newspaper reporter snapped a few pictures of Weyou, pitifully lying there, stuck in the Thanelep Ride. He did not smile for the camera. He was very embarrassed.

His big brother came out and taunted him. "Weyou's in trouble, Weyou's in trouble," he chanted. He looked at the coin slot return. "Hey, here's a quadzep!" he said with delight. He took the silver quadzep and put it in his pocket. Weyou thought about saying it was his quadzep, but just let it go. "Too bad for you, Weyou. You're in big trouble now!" Alackh ran back into the store. The Fire Chief came up and looked at Weyou's wedged arm.

"Do you think we gotta cut him out of there?" said the store clerk.

The scaly, wise, experienced Fire Chief winked his bigger eye, twirled his big braided mustache and said "No, I think we can get him out of there pretty easy, you betcha." He went back to the engine and got out a slime gun. He squeezed some slime into his palm and came back to Weyou. He put the slime around Weyou's elbow and jiggled it a little. Then, he pulled and Weyou's tentacle popped out of the crevice, waving freely in the air. Weyou was free at last. The crowd applauded. The Fire Chief winked all three eyes and got in the fire engine and took off. It was all over. Weyou was okay, with just a small bruise. Embarrassed, his Mom angrily grabbed his tentacle and dragged him back to the car, and they drove home. Weyou noticed that Alackh had an ice cream cone.

"Can I have an ice cream cone?' he asked, plaintively.

"No!" said Mom, looking over her shoulder at him in the back seat. "You don't deserve it! You've been a bad boy, a very bad boy! I'm never taking you here again!" She turned her great horned head away from him, pointedly.

Weyou cried now. The waterworks came on, full blast. He cried and cried, the slime streaming down his red cheeks, dripping onto his shirt. He was a Slime Baby. He didn't care who knew it. He sobbed and howled and blubbered and bawled and bellowed and shrieked and wailed and keened. His nose slots snotted up and slimed as he gasped for air between each cry. His suction cups got slimy and stuck to the seats, so he couldn't wipe his slime. He cried like the biggest slime baby there ever was, all the way home. Alackh, in the front seat turned around to Weyou and said "Ha-Ha!" and stuck out his long forked tongue to lick the ice cream he held in one suction cup. With his third tentacle, he dangled a black rubber razzbiter on an elastic string at him.

The Dark Spaceship

The planet Aed'n has never been set foot on. Humans have no idea about what could possibly live there, but I do, so I'll tell you all about it.

I'm the only human to ever survive. My story isn't like anyone else's and my life, well, a lot of girls lose interest when they find out who my mom is.

When I was an infant, the interspace hospital I was born at was taken over by a species of rebel aliens. To make a long story short, I somehow ended up going out the garbage chute and floating around in space for a few days, until I floated down to a planet, to meet my fate. As a tiny baby, that's pretty scary, but the aliens who raised me, I think they did a good job. Minus the few times I woke up over a fire.

Anyways, my mom is the oldest alien to ever live. She was actually once a queen. She was on a mission and halfway through her journey, her spacecraft was hit by an asteroid and ended up being stranded on this planet. She only had two other aliens with her, Pork and Yeila. Pork was her bodyguard, I guess you'd call it. He's the youngest, but back home, he was really strong. Yeila is my mom's friend. She is the second oldest alien in existence, but she looks younger than Pork.

Yeila was the one who taught me English, she taught all of us English. Pork taught me how to play with space rocks and my mom, whose name is Thaedni, she is the calmest of all of us, also the wisest and the quietest.

Today though, is just like any other day, well it started out that way. I was pacing around, thinking about not wanting to eat coral again and this bright light appeared in the sky. None of us knew what it was. It came closer and we all just stared in awe. It was a ship! A space ship and it was landing on our planet; what would a space ship be doing on our planet? We hardly have any water or food or anything that would make this planet appealing. Maybe they've come to rescue us, sure took them long enough.

Anyways, the ship landed with quite the thud, stirring up a lot space dust and making only me cough. The odd thing was, no one ever came out of the ship. When nightfall came, no lights went on in the ship. It simply sat there. It was eerie looking, but Pork wanted to investigate it anyways. Thaedni forbid any of us from even going near it, and got nervous if any

94

of us even looked at it for too long. All day and into the night the ship sat there. If I had only known then what I knew now, I would've made Pork, Yeila, Thaedni and I, run for the hills and fast.

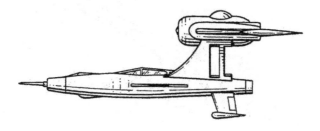

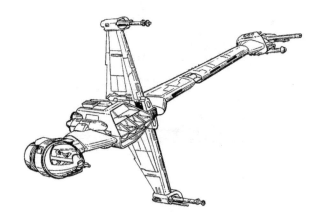

Why There Are No Aliens from Outer Space

by J. P. Cloud

"Professor! Professor! Please wait, sir! I want to talk to you!" called the young student. The Professor smiled and held up, glad that there was an inquisitive student he could further educate. "I heard your lecture, sir, and wanted to ask you. Don't you believe that there is really intelligent life in the Universe?" asked the boy.

"Yes, I don't" said the Professor.

"But, sir! You mean, you don't believe in aliens from outer space?"

"No."

"Do you mean to say, that out of all the billions of stars and galaxies, you don't believe in intelligent life out there?"

"No, I don't believe so."

"How can you be so sure?"

"I know there is no intelligent life out there, and I'm not so sure about down here, either!" He smiled. "I'm just joking. But there is no intelligent life up there."

"In the whole Universe?"

"The whole Universe."

"But what about all the evidence?"

The Professor snorted. "There is no evidence, my boy. There's no proof of aliens from outer space. It's all just folklore, hallucinations or hoaxes. There was never any solid proof. Not even a good photo or video. You would think with everyone having access to cameras and videos these days, that there would be volumes of photos and film of them. But to this day, there is not even one. With all the so-called close encounters and alien abductions, there is still not one dead alien found."

"Dead?"

"Yes, dead. If the aliens were here, we would have found a dead one. We haven't found a dead one. That's because there aren't any. There never were."

"What about the Ancient Aliens theory?"

"It's just that, a theory. A story. A very good story, but just a story. More folklore. Besides, the aliens, if they existed, could never make it to this planet."

"Why not?"

"They would be much too far away. It would take many thousands of years to get here, even if they did manage to build a spacecraft capable of going light-speed. Sentient beings cannot live for thousands of years. Maybe moss, or lichens, or gases, but no living intelligent beings."

"What if there really were other worlds out there? There must be!"

"What if? What if? What if angels danced on the heads of pins?" He shook his old, gray head. "No. We'd detect them. If there were any inhabited planets within our galaxy and beyond, we would have detected them. And they'd have to follow our planet's Laws of Physics. Our planet's science isn't perfect, but it's pretty darn good. It's all speculation." He pointed up into the clear night sky. "Do you see that big bright star up there? The one that's just off the handle of the Big Dipper?"

"Yes, I see it," said the boy. "It's twinkling with colors."

"That was what was known as a Gas Giant. At one time, it had nine uninhabited planets circling around it. It was a beautiful star."

"Was, sir?"

"Yes, was. It's not there anymore."

"But I see it, right there!"

"No, it's not there. What you see is the way it looked one million years ago. That gas giant was one million light years away. The light you see took one million years to get here. The star exploded a half a million years ago.

You are seeing it before it exploded. It's a good thing none of those planets were inhabited, because any living beings there would have frozen to death, if they did survive the heat from the explosion."

"That's amazing!" The boy was truly impressed. "I never thought about that!"

"No one does, unless you know about astronomy, like I do. You are actually looking back into the past, many thousands of years ago, with your own eyes. Most of the brightest stars you see up there right now are gone. They don't exist anymore."

"That's incredible! It's almost scary, sir."

"Yes, it is. It makes you realize how insignificant we all really are. Light travels at 480,000 miles per hour. Can some being make a spacecraft that could go that fast? Can some being live for a million years, much less a thousand?" He looked at the student.

"No, sir."

"Then you see what I mean. For all intents and purposes, there are no alien beings out there."

"What about time warps, or folds in space? What about dimensional rifts?"

"Again, only speculation. Fedlohn admits it. Ragan admits it. Ragan thinks there might be aliens, but I don't. It makes for a nice story, though. But don't believe me!" he chuckled. "Ask any astrophysicist, like Professor Radlor. It's all basic stuff."

"I… I just can't believe…out of all the billions and billions of stars up there…that there are no other inhabited planets, with intelligent life," said the boy, disheartened.

The Professor wrapped a slimy tentacle around the boy. "My boy, I can see you are very intelligent. I can see that you crave knowledge and the truth. But the real truth is there is no intelligent life in the Universe. It's all nonsense. Folklore. Hoax. Nothing more. You must listen to me. I know what I'm talking about, I'm a scientist. Now run along to your classes and forget all about this nonsense."

"Yes, Professor. Thank you for your wise words. Goodbye, sir."

"Goodbye, my boy."

CPSIA information can be obtained
at www.ICGtesting.com
Printed in the USA
FSHW012016040620
70924FS